# DISASTER
# WAITING

*A Modern Day Parable about a
Modern Day Dilemma*

## AC CURTIS

WESTBOW®
PRESS
A DIVISION OF THOMAS NELSON
& ZONDERVAN

Scripture quotations taken from the Holy Bible, New Living Translation, copyright 1996, 2004. Used by permission of Tyndale House Publishers, Inc., Wheaton, Illinois 60189. All rights reserved.

WestBow Press books may be ordered through booksellers or by contacting:

WestBow Press
A Division of Thomas Nelson & Zondervan
1663 Liberty Drive
Bloomington, IN 47403
www.westbowpress.com
1 (866) 928-1240

Because of the dynamic nature of the Internet, any web addresses or links contained in this book may have changed since publication and may no longer be valid. The views expressed in this work are solely those of the author and do not necessarily reflect the views of the publisher, and the publisher hereby disclaims any responsibility for them.

Any people depicted in stock imagery provided by Thinkstock are models, and such images are being used for illustrative purposes only. Certain stock imagery © Thinkstock.

ISBN: 978-1-4908-2524-3 (sc)
ISBN: 978-1-4908-2525-0 (e)

Library of Congress Control Number: 2014902039

Printed in the United States of America.

WestBow Press rev. date: 01/31/2014

# DISASTER WAITING
## – PART I

# Chapter One

# STORM APPROACHING

*From the National Weather Service:*

*The National Weather Service has issued a severe thunderstorm warning for the following counties in North-eastern Alabama and North Georgia. This system is expected to bring tornados and major flash flooding for the counties in its path, with estimates of up to 16 inches of rain. All residents are advised to move to higher elevation and travel advisories are in place.*

This was it – the day that Maria Temple had anticipated. She looked out of her kitchen window anxiously waiting to see her husband, Don striding up the cobble stoned pathway that led to their back door in charming Birmingham, Alabama. As she spotted him, she met her husband with a commanding hug that sent him back a few steps. She wasn't going to let this moment slip away.

Don came home to his wife, Maria, their two sons, Zack and Ben, and their daughter Brea. He had just finished another grueling day at work and was now ready to start a two-week hiatus away from his office in downtown Birmingham and into the serene beauty of Lookout Mountain, Georgia. It was the highly anticipated vacation Maria had been contending for in the eight years she and Don had been married, and nothing was going to detour them from this opportunity. The dream of being together as a family combined with the ambience of crisp mountain air and starlit evenings was only eclipsed by the energetic anticipation of the rugged adventures ahead. After all, they had worked for months on preparing and saving for the "vacation of a lifetime" that would include back packing, camping, and plenty of nights without TV, I-phones, Twitter, daily planners, or constant arguing over the bills and the kids.

Now, it was time, it was their time. Nothing was going to keep them away.

"Oh, I can't wait to smell that fresh mountain air and feel the wind in my face!" squealed Maria with excitement.

"Yeah, and reelin in that ten pounder with Zack right by my side in the boat," added Don.

"This is gonna be one to remember," Maria sighed heavily.

"So, are you finally done or you think Larry's gonna throw you another curve ball like he did last year?" Maria prodded as Don slumped down into the more-than-comfortable recliner.

Don was worn-out from an over-indulgence in work and yet elated at the idea of two weeks away from the insurance company that had bargained away most of his time since he and Maria married and started having children. Their lives seemed full of consistent chaos as they worked hard each week to keep both a roof over their heads and a sense of peace, and still they never seemed to save enough to put away for that "rainy day" – until now.

"Is Daddy home yet Mama?" asked Zack, the oldest and the most rugged adventurer in the house.

"Yes, sweety, and what does that mean?" Maria cheerfully taunted.

"It means we're goin to the mountains!" Zack shouted as he ran excitedly back to tell his sister Brea. It was also his duty to help little Ben, his two-year old brother, to get his shoes on the right feet.

"You know, I'm ready too, and it's about time," said Don as he sprang confidently out of the chair and back to his feet. "And why not, after all even the McCormick's got to go on vacation last month. I decided then that we needed to do this."

"That's what I love about you – that take charge attitude" teased Maria. "Oh, and while you're getting the van ready with your take-charge self, take charge of that stinky trash can as well. Last thing we need is two week-old smelling trash to welcome us back in the door."

"I guess I can use these 'guns' (referring admirably to his biceps) for taking charge *and* taking trash" exclaimed Don resolutely.

"Why not just use your fading glories (referring not so admirably to his aforementioned biceps) to take out the cooler as well, Mr. Incredible?" Maria teased further.

With the children scurrying around trying to find toys for the road trip and Maria applying the finishing touches on the road-munchies bag, the family was soon loaded into the minivan and winding their way down the narrow curved pathway leading away from their house and into a the long-awaited vacation-paradise.

"Have you heard the weather report honey?" asked Maria nervously. "I heard it's looking nasty up where we're goin.'"

"I checked it. Some are saying its cuttin'up like a room full-o-chain saws, while others are saying it's a stalled system and moving north toward Kentucky." speculated Don. "Relax though, honey, I'm sure nothin's gonna spoil out dream vacation. And heck, we're Temples! We can make it through anything!"

Weather reports indeed had been issued alarming travelers of the impending system. Forecasters in the Alabama and Georgia area had expressed deep concern that flash flooding might occur especially in the Chattanooga Valley area directly where Lookout Mountain was located. Undaunted, the Temple family was determined to go through with their plans. The family took off for the 270 mile journey toward excitement.

And though for the time excitement was the prevailing mood, no one could know tumultuous danger that was about to encroach upon their lives, such danger that would test their resolve and push them past the point of exhaustion and despair, leaving them clinging to a thread of life and very little hope. Disaster was waiting for the Temples. Would they see it in time? Would they have the courage to get through it? Would they perish?

Still to come? The unthinkable.

The thick, dark clouds were already rolling in hanging over the horizon like a black crepe. The Pine Mountain area, though breathtakingly beautiful, looked poised for an immediate downpour, ominously signaling the massive approaching storm. Though thunderstorms were common, the Enhanced Fujita Scale and Weather Radars in the area were predicting mass destruction from this system. Straight-line winds were expected to peak at 60-70 miles per hour carrying up to 16 or more inches of rain. To one man, Brock Dunbar, this storm reminded him of some of the worst he had seen in his long and storied past. Brock gazed at the sky with investigative wonder. His trained intuition served him well so many times in these situations, and though he was in a hurry to get back to headquarters in South Georgia, Brock couldn't help but think that he might be stuck in the *North* Georgia area for some time.

"Lookin pretty bleak" he noted as he stared at the upcoming storm trying to gather clues to the intensity of the situation. "Ay, ya wicked Sally, ya aint gonna get the best of ol Brock though, nah ya aint."

Brock, a ruggedly-built, 58 year old southern man with Scotch-Irish roots had been the enigmatic, yet stable Incident Commander of an elite National Search and Rescue team called SAR Alpha for over 30 years. In fact, he had been the original architect of the team that had participated in over 4,800 search and rescue missions all over the United States. This team had experienced little to no personnel turnover in the thirty years that Brock was leader. However, recently Team Alpha had key team members retire and move on. Brock was left, therefore, to patch up the holes in personnel and to find quality mission-team members that could follow easily in his footsteps. The recent process had made Brock swear off the hard stuff many times and caused more than his share of headaches.

With his SAR (Search and Rescue) 24-hour kit bag slung over his burly shoulders, Brock jumped onto his 4-wheeler and sped back through the woods toward his truck. He was preparing himself to make the executive decision to stay put in the area figuring that, despite the Team's repositioning, SAR Alpha would be needed soon. The call came seconds into his self-debating.

"Alpha Base to Alpha 1. Alpha Base to Alpha 1, do you copy?"

"Alpha 1 – go ahead."

"Alpha 1, we are sending your team into position there in Pine Mountain on Red Alert now. Copy?"

"Copy. I figgered ya was gonna since this thing's lookin nasty. When are they expected, Alpha Base?"

"Within the hour, Alpha 1, you should expect them soon – good luck with this team Brock, they're good, they're talented, but they're not you. Alpha Base over and out."

"Ah, guess we'll see who's gonna treat me worse, this storm or this team. It's time to do your thang, Brock ol boy."

Brock was predicting the usual winsome welcome by his K-9 special operations dogs, Trooper and Bullseye, and in all probability, a not-so-amiable reception from his newly-formed team members. The new recruits would have to get used to him, his leadership, and the manner in which Team Alpha conducted its business. Brock was in the rescuing business, not the recruitment business, and he knew that "Search and Rescue Operations" left no room for error or compromise, even if it meant he might have to devote some time to whipping some of the team into shape. This was his stand and this was the door that was now opened to a new generation of emboldened rescuers. All the pleasantries aside, Brock was ready to give this new recruitment class their personal crash course in reality. The reality check for him would come later.

This was shaping up to be an adventure he would never forget.

Valerie Caldwell, an ambitious marketing firm director from upstate New York, couldn't be happier with her new job opportunity and her new lease on life. She had gone through a very arduous special Red Cross training and then, after serving 4 years as a volunteer with NorthEast Search and Rescue Team (NEMSAR), she began submitting her application to whoever might "call back". This was as drastic of a career change as she had ever initiated, but it was worth it. Valerie had grown tired of the topsy-turvy situation with her ex-husband, Richard, and her new boyfriend, Carl. On one hand, Richard was constantly bugging her about her personal life and her professional life though they had been divorced for 3 years. She just couldn't get him out of her life no matter how hard she tried.

Carl, on the other hand, needed to finally make up his mind and settle down with her for good. She had deep romantic feelings for him but had not tamed him yet. His wishy-washy behavior was leading her to give it all up and join a nunnery instead of a rescue team.

Amazingly, Valerie received the "call-back" from a dear friend who knew Brock Dunbar personally. He had pushed for her application to be accepted and… despite some reservation on Brock's part, she was finally suiting up ready to join the elite Team Alpha. For now, it was time to try to leave her "men-problems" behind. The challenges ahead with this new team would loom more menacing than arbitrating between Richard and Carl on any given stage.

Today, Valerie waited in nervous anticipation, along with the other new team-members, to finally meet the legendary Brock Dunbar. She had heard so many stories and felt a bit like a child again as she wondered which of those stories about Brock could possibly be true. She also wondered if Brock would be able to work with her at all. Maybe time would tell.

Jeb Tanner, from Newburry, South Carolina, was an athletic supernova who breezed through preliminary training and acceptance levels of Team Alpha like a knife going through hot butter. Jeb had been a standout captain on the Clemson football team as well as a three-sport star there. He ran a 4.5 - 40 and was timed just as fast with his mouth as he frequently publicized his accomplishments to those who would or would not listen. Although copiously impertinent, Jeb was good at his job. He had served admirably with the Search Tactics Rescue and Recovery of South Carolina (S.T.A.R.R) for 6 years before landing this new gig. His record with S.T.A.R.R would have been flawless except for the constant "heroic exhibitions" which would keep his team in a constant revolving door of members. This got him suspended from S.T.A.R.R but picked up by Team Alpha.

Although super confident of personally impressing Brock, Jeb felt a twinge of anxiety as he talked it up with Valerie on their way to headquarters. Jeb and Valerie were meeting the other new recruits and sparks were sure to fly. Skylar Townsend, Tim Cohen, Sabrina Carlson, and Jared Petti, mainly known as Jag, would be joining Valerie and Jeb as the newest members of one of the most successful and disciplined Search and Rescue Teams in the nation.

Their stories and experiences were as varied as their talents. These stories as well as their talents would be needed much more than they would realize in the immediate 24 hours that lay ahead.

Skylar, a tall, thin young rescuer had been a rigging specialist with the very high-ranking Douglas County Search and Rescue Team from Colorado, his home state. As great as he was in performance, he lost more ground in the past due to his overt attitude of self-preservation. When called upon to do a job, there was none better, as long as he would be out of harm's way. When he acted out his usual manner, while on a rescue operation in the Rocky Mountains, his team "voted him off the island", so to speak, by giving him his easy ticket toward the exit door of that elite SAR Unit. Shortly thereafter, Skylar went to work with a construction firm and then began reapplying with rescue units in his area. He applied with Team Alpha five times until finally accepted. He was given this new opportunity at Search and Rescue redemption and given a chance to utilize his skills while putting a lid on his propensity to dodge danger. Danger would prove to be his greatest friend when all was said and done.

Tim, a ruddy, impressive, and super-intelligent young man from Emerson City, Illinois, had excelled for 8 years as an airman in the US Air Force. Tim had also served with the highly esteemed Civil Air Patrol of Scott Air Force Base in Illinois. He won countless awards for excellence in academics and was a genius with gadgetry. Wherever he went he carried his computer with him and his "trouble-shooter" bag filled with parts from hundreds of gadgets that most people threw away. Tim was the logistical director on his rescue team back home. Despite his overwhelming talents, Tim was a perfectionist and had always publicly hinted of being given the role of leading his own team. His private abhorrence of leadership would often cause him to spill out venom toward his team leadership in public, drastically undermining team effectiveness and order. His incessant open questioning of the tactics and motives of his leaders cost him dearly. Now, however, he had an opportunity at "rescue redemption" - with Team Alpha. It would become the catalyst between decision and denial for Tim in the waning hours of the upcoming rescue operation.

Jared Petti was best known by his nickname, Jag. Jag had been a logistics team leader for most of his six-year career in Search and Rescue work. Put a clip-board and rescue team equipment in his care and there was none better. He was also renowned for his ability to turn any situation into a stand-up comedy act. Where others might run from a social gathering, Jag was sprinting toward the crowd. Hailing from Lincoln, Nebraska, Jag was more venerated by his peers in Lincoln than the Cornhusker mascot from Nebraska University. Despite his favorable demeanor, Jag's mouth often got him trouble and he often showed a propensity to miss the seriousness of the situation – not so good when your very vocation requires the utmost in seriousness. Despite this, Jag had served well on his rescue team in Nebraska, the Nebraska Urban Search and Rescue Team (NUSAR) based right from his home town. Now, he was looking forward to a fresh start with Team Alpha, hoping to make an instant splash with the renowned, Brock Dunbar, before anyone else on the team could muscle him out.

Sabrina Carlson, a naturalist who worked at NUSAR along with Jag in Nebraska, had jumped at the opportunity to join Jag in a new prestigious career and so applied along with him. Though extremely industrious in her efforts, Sabrina had been a thorn in the side of all efforts to build chemistry on her former team in Lincoln, highlighting a very inconspicuous nature to find the negative in most situations. She had grown up as a ward of the Lincoln Courts and was tossed back and forth from foster home to foster home as a child. Though she meant well, she could not help finding herself looking, not at the silver lining of any situation, but always the dark side of even the best. This would prove nearly fatal for her indoctrination into "team-hood" aboard the USS Brock Dunbar Express. It would also prove to play a huge role later in her inability to cope with an experience that would challenge everyone to the core of courage and team dependency.

The repartee of team interfacing would have to wait, Brock just arrived.

The door flung open with sudden force as the large assuming figure came bursting through with a commanding presence that made the excited atmosphere of the room become abruptly tense and sublimely subdued. Brock was here to get ready to weed out any malcontents on this new Team Alpha rookie squad while getting them ready quickly for the task staring them in the face there in North Georgia. He hardly wasted a second to begin taunting and subtly tenderizing the new personnel.

"Ay, ya wicked sallies, I guess you're the bunch that made it through training?" he inquired somewhat sarcastically. "Now how the heck are we supposed to rescue anyone with this ragtag group?" "Man alive, they keep sendin me *rejects* when I ask for *recruits!*"

Though Brock's caustic manner kept him from an endearing first impression, still one of the recruits, Jag, decided to jump on the chance to show off superior confidence first.

"Yeah, we're it captain. Guess you won't be rescuin' too many kittens out of trees from this group, huh?"

"No, and I guess it's good since it's never been kittens that we're goin after!" retorted Brock as he shut the door behind him with a bang. "I can see we're gonna have fun with you, ya wicked sally. So, what's your name?"

"Names Jag" he answered. "I'm the total package when it comes to bein a supa-savin-grabbin-life by the …"

In order to not be outshined, Jeb suddenly interrupted, saying, "Hey, old man, me and the Jagsman are the best you got and we can handle anything you shell out."

"Oh yeah, is that a fact?" Brock rebutted.

"Yeah, Delta-Force baby!" bragged Jeb.

"More like Delta-Farce," joked Brock.

"Bet you're gonna be surprised when it's all said and done," quipped Jag.

"Let's hope, *pleasantly* surprised," answered Brock with a hint of hopefulness.

"Bam! There it is!" interjected Jeb. "Jag and I were born to do this. So, point us in the right direction old-timer, and we'll show you our stuff!" he bragged.

"That self-confidence may come in handy" said Brock. "But we'd better not stay around and chat on your level too much longer. We have work to do."

"Already? What's up?" asked Skylar. "More training?"

"I wish it were, but looks like you're gonna be hittin the ground runnin" Brock announced.

"Yeah, we were wondering about that as Alpha Base got us packed and ready in a hurry" added Valerie.

"Well, as of 1400 hours, we have confirmed reports that due to the storm system in North Georgia, many towns around the Pine Mountain Resort area are already under "flash flood" status. So far the levies are holding but

I've just received orders to dispatch this team to that area by 1500 hours to be boots ready and on the ground." acknowledged Brock.

"We'll be ready cap, more ready than a cat in a room full of yarn!" quipped Jag.

"Ten minutes, you each have just ten minutes!" Brock ordered sharply. "Double-check your gear and get to the chopper. Don't forget to cross-check with each other. Check all Prusiks! Red lines with red lines. Belays in every bag. Go with the auto-locking caribiners. Oh, yeah, and one more thing…"

"Yeah Cap, what is it?" Valerie asked.

"Don't fall over your rookie selves. I need you all for my retirement plaque at the end of all this."

"Oh, so you want us to make you look good – right?" Valerie went on.

"Yup, just don't forget that sister and you might make it outta there in one piece," Brock retorted.

With the preliminaries out of the way, the team hurried to the situation room to get their gear and briefing on communications and logistics. They would have to go in with the water rising at a historical rate and each hour might be the difference between life, death, and even massive destruction.

Directly at 1410 hours, Team Alpha was geared up and on their way, moving quickly to the team's helicopter pad heading into the unknown.

As they boarded the H-19 Rescue Chopper, Brock's thoughts were haunted by his earlier intuition of his new team's readiness. He had wanted more time to acclimate the new recruits into his "way of doing things". Thoughts quickly morphed into questions: "Could this team merge their training, their abilities and their experiences in time? Would they be like the teams he led before – *on time, on target, on task?*"

These nagging questions were punishing Brock's mind. He has seen so much in his lifetime. So many lives had been rescued in the past, but now, his footing was unsure, his bearings not so secure and, to top it all off – his "darned hand was hurting like the dickens from that blamed arthritis!" The guys back at HQ should know what he was up against on this one. If only he had some of the overachievers he had worked with in the past. They could help fortify his resolve with much-needed confidence and really get the mess cleaned up!

But, all of that would have to wait. Now it was time to see, not only what *they* were made of, but what *he* and *his leadership* were made of. Disaster was right around the corner. The team would have to muster not only courage but unity in the face of disaster. Team Alpha would have to galvanize quickly! Would they come out as heroes? Would they come out at all?

Answers were right around the corner.

# Chapter Two

# DISASTER STRIKES

"Don, it's looking real bad up ahead. Are you sure we shouldn't just get a hotel at the next exit and spend the night?" Maria nervously asked.

"Hey, it was you who stayed on my back to get reservations for this chalet. I had to give a $200 non-refundable deposit for it," Don snapped back. "Anyway, the kids are asleep and we only have another hour and a half to go, maybe two. We can make it to the chalet in time and get bedded down for the night. You'll see."

"Hey, I just want to get somewhere safe and quick!" Maria jabbed. "Let's just get there and get out of this. You know how I feel about driving in storms."

"Alright, I'm sorry Maria. I just want you to see I'm trying my best," Don replied as he continued eastward.

The rain and wind beat against the van with near hurricane force for two anxious hours. Finally, the Temples arrived in Pine Mountain Resort Lodge to check into their reserved chalet. The young clerk at the front desk seemed nervous but unsympathetic, and even less encouraging.

"Ya'll sure are brave!" he exclaimed to the Temples. "We had plenty of cancellations. This storm is a-tearin thangs up pretty bad and the river is reeeeeally startin to rise! Ya sure you want the room?"

"We're here aren't we?!?" Maria replied trying to gain self-confidence and maintain control at the same time.

"Well ok, ma'am, just want you to be reassured that, in the event of rising water, your deposit can be returned after the proper paper-work is filled out and sent in," the clerk replied reading parts of his reply from a sign posted behind his desk.

"Oh, that's reassuring, thanks," Maria sarcastically replied.

"Dear, it's going to be ok, let's just get in and get these kids down for the night," interjected her husband.

The Temple's chalet was as beautiful and spacious as anything they had ever seen but was located at the bottom of a steep, dirt route that wound ruthlessly around a narrow path right up to the banks of the river. Though worn from the road trip and especially the last two hours, the family nestled into their quaint home away from home to try to get some much-needed sleep, and mostly… wait out the worst.

The worst was not what they could have imagined.

"I'm so scared Daddy!" Brea cried as Don tucked her into bed. "What if that mean ol water comes up to us and washes us away?"

"There's nothing to fear tonight. There are things called levies that hold back the river. They are doing their job and you are going to do yours tonight sweetie, get some sleep. You need it. Daddy loves his little Breesum."

"Daddy, do you ever feel scared?" asked Brea admiring her Daddy.

"You know, Breesum, there have been many times in Daddy's life when I felt scared," Don answered warmly as he sat beside her at the foot of the bed. "When I was in the navy, before you were born, I well remember a time off the coast of Kuwait when, during a port of call, we started getting shelled from above by the Republican Guard Air Force of Iraq. We were there as part of a major coalition to oust the tyrant Hussein in Iraq. Our ship was backing the F-14 Tomcats conducting MIGCAP missions in an effort to turn back enemy fighters. Suddenly, a squadron of bogeys got through our Tomcat lines and started pelting our ship with major ferocity."

"The sky was dark and … oh, sorry sweetie, bet you didn't understand much of that I just said," Don interjected.

"It's ok, Daddy," Brea said sleepily with eyes barely open. "You always do that when you're talking about your days in the Navy. I know 'cause you always get that look in your eyes like you wish you were back on that ship again," she added affectionately.

"You, my little princess, are just waaaayyy too smart for your age!" Don laughed. "Now, let me tuck you in and let you get started on dreaming about our wonderful vacation. And, besides, I thought I carried you in here asleep already!"

Don closed the door quietly behind him and walked toward the front room where the boys were. He placed his hand on Ben, his young 4 year old son, sighing serenely at the notion of a good night's sleep for his worn-out youngster, then turned to Zack, his growing 11 year old first-born son.

"Hey broheem, how's this trip so far for you?" he asked hoping for some positive reassurance.

"Dad, despite the weather, I think things are shaping up great!" Zack answered quickly

"Well, I, for one, cannot wait to hook that bass with you and little Ben tomorrow!" Don replied with excitement.

"Me too Dad. Me too. Hey, do I get to put the bait on the hook myself this time?" Zack asked relying on past fishing excursion experiences with his dad.

"You betcha dude! You are ready for that now. Heck, you're practically a man already!" Don replied.

Don kissed Zack on the forehead and walked out of the room with renewed personal confidence that his family might have fun after all.

He headed back to the master bedroom to finally get to bed and dry off a bit.

"Honey, I know I said we need to stay tonight, but was that desk clerk for real? Will the river keep rising?" Maria prodded.

"Honey, you know I don't know for sure, but I do know that the levies are in place. I checked online and did my research a bit before the trip. Are you suggesting…?"

"Not suggesting anything honey, not yet. I know you've worked hard for us and I really appreciate you Don. There's no man like you. And, I know you can't control or know everything. I guess it's always good to hear your confidence and I didn't hear it tonight."

"I know," Don replied trying to reassure Maria of his excellent preparedness in the situation. "I really hope things will be ok, and part of me wants to keep going on with this vacation that we've worked so hard for and the other part of me is screaming out that we need to *bail* on it."

"Let's just hope we don't have to *"bail"* water out – no pun intended," Maria answered.

After a few minutes of continued speculation, the happy, but weather-worn couple finally went to sleep, hoping that the worst case scenario would never happen to them.

The worst case scenario, in fact, was exactly what was headed their way.

The river was rising each hour. The levies holding much of the rushing water were giving way in the middle of the night. Engulfed in water, the chalet that was supposed to offer much-needed respite would soon offer only disaster. Death, like a dream, would suddenly creep up on the Temple family, and, like a waiting Boa Constrictor, the raging river would be ready to squeeze out the life and dreams of this family, plunging each of them into a nightmare that would take a miracle to survive.

Suddenly, the water came rushing in.

"Dad! Dad! Wake up!" yelled Zack as he pulled on his Dad's shirt trying to get him out of bed. Ben and Brea were screaming in the back room and the bed was floating.

"Oh my God!" yelled Don. "We're floating away!"

Maria woke up screaming as Don waded through the waist-high water toward the children who were huddled together on the bed in the other room. He worked his way frantically toward the bed snatching up Ben and Brea and wading back toward Zack and Maria.

"Hurry, take my hand, we have to get out quick!" he yelled.

The family quickly made their way toward the front door of the chalet. At that precise moment a wall of water came rushing like a bullet toward the family at break-neck speed catapulting each of them away from each other and down into a maddening undertow.

Don frantically made his way to the top of the torrent. "Maria! Maria! Zack! Oh my God please help me! Help me!"

Just then out of the water popped Zack's head followed quickly by Brea and Maria. They were all gasping uncontrollably but alive, paddling to stay afloat for as long as possible.

"Where's Ben? Ben! Ben!" screamed Maria frantically.

Each of them paddled around screaming out the name of their 2 year old – Ben. Though dazed by the shock of what was happening, Don and Maria knew they had to act fast. Don dove back down into the rushing waters swimming and begging. "Oh God please help me find my Ben!"

Don popped up out of the water again and again, over and over. Maria dove as well but could not hold long. Suddenly, Don spotted a huge rock a few feet away from all of them.

"Everyone - swim over there - now!" he yelled pointing to the rock. Maria helped Brea over as Zack swam as fast as he could over to the rock to help his mom and sister. Don kept after the search for Ben diving over and over into the rushing waters. Exhausted, he kept the search going on adrenaline only.

"I'm gonna try downstream a bit. Stay there on the rock!"

"Find my baby, please don't give up Don!" screamed Maria.

Don swam and dipped down into the swollen river over and over until his body went completely out of sight swallowed up quickly by the unforgiving water.

"Don! Oh my God, Don!" screamed Maria again and again.

"Daddy! Come back Daddy!" screamed Brea. "Come back!"

Zack held onto the rock and his sister, breathing each breath with a prayer, begging God to save them all.

Each of them lay desperate and helpless in the rushing river holding on to the rock and losing hope that they would ever see Don and Ben again.

Hope would have a name – Team Alpha.

# Chapter Three

# TIME TO RESCUE!

Team Alpha had arrived on the scene of the worst flood to hit the area in 100 years. The entire River Basin was covered with water up to the rooftops of chalets. There was no time to waste, very little time even to get down to the river.

"Dang, it's worse than I imagined!" reacted Brock as he and his team surveyed the flooded river in the ravine. "We're gonna' have to get in there. The river is racing through and the towns around are already taking on water faster than a dog after a meat bone," he added.

"Oh my gosh, I just knew it! Why did it happen on my first day?" complained Sabrina. "Looks like a total wasted area!" she continued. "I'll tell you there may not be anything or anyone alive in that ravine at all. Least I don't know how there could be.

"Well, guess we can all go home then," joked Jag. "Nothin' could've survived all that mess!"

"What a beast you are!" scolded Valerie. "Just like a man, finding some kind of joke out of all this."

"Well you want me to just go down there and pull everyone out myself?" retorted Jag.

"What happened to you and Jeb being Delta Force?" she screamed back.

"Shut up you two. This is not the time for any of your junk" yelled Brock. "It's time to get busy. There are people down there needing our help."

"What's the game plan Cap?" asked Jeb.

"First of all, we have to assess the immediate and scan the perimeters in order to seal off and determine our target area. I imagine this river basin will be climbin' with rescue teams. So far, though, we're the first," answered Brock.

The team rushed toward the Pine Mountain ravine where the greatest damage from the flood seemed to be. To their immediate astonishment, there appeared to be no one in danger. They still had much of the river to survey, however, so the trek was on, each of them carrying necessary gear and anticipating a long-day's work as they boarded their fully-packed Land Rover.

What would they find? Would they be able to work together to rescue if they did?

"I tell you what, if I were putting in to the river I'd use a zip-line with this new carabiner I made in a hurry" Tim blurted out. "Although, I doubt Val could get from the top of a tree on a zip-line if she had to," he said half-teasing.

"Just you stick with what works for you, pig!" Valerie yelled back.

"Hey, what's up Val?" he recoiled. "I was just kiddin'"

"I'm just sayin', I came up with a brand new idea for a carabiner that hooks up more than one person at a time. Heck, even Sabrina could figure it out!" Tim self-congratulated.

"Val's right – you *are* a pig!" Sabrina retorted disgustingly.

"That's why I didn't want to take this job, working with slugs like you guys. All you think about is yourself. Think I'll stick with Sabrina," chimed in Valerie.

Seeing any semblance of unity quickly evaporating before his eyes, Brock opened up quickly barking out - "Hey guys, what's up? This is the team we gotta' work with and I think I'll be the one pairing ya'll up, not you!"

"That's right – preach it!" Skylar added.

"And who cranked your chain?" asked Valerie, looking to silence another male voice on the team.

"Hey, I'm not in this with you sis, just keep quiet and do your job. I'm not here for you anyway. I'm here for me. So, stay out of my way!" reacted Skylar.

The verbal assaults were suddenly put on hold when someone spotted a moving body in the water.

"There's one!" Jag yelled, pointing to the huge rock in the middle of the raging river.

"Not one, looks like three" said Jeb.

"Let's get over there quick! Grab the rope and prusiks, get ready to hook up the carabiners, and get down there now!" barked Brock.

Team Alpha moved into position toward the rock that Maria, Zack, and Brea were clinging to. They hooked up and sent JAG, Brock and Skylar down with the rest of the team holding them.

"Hook 'em up. Hold steady. Now move!" Brock ordered.

Jag arrived first.

"Ma'am, are you ok? Are you hurt at all? We're here to get you out. You'll need to grab my hand as I hold this locking pin in place," he commanded as he was assaulted violently by the rushing water.

Jag locked the anchor plate in position attaching the ropes and vests onto Maria and the children.

"Get the children first!" Maria yelled shivering and trying to raise her voice over the noise of the rushing waters and her own exhaustion.

"Hook up the little one!" Skylar yelled.

The three of them hooked up the children and Maria and began hoisting them toward the shore using the Hi-Line Carriage pulley Tim had brought. As they brought the Temples closer to shore it seemed that each minute was like an hour, as the water splashed against them with juggernaut force. At one point, Brock could feel his fingers slipping from the Bluewater Safeline Rope he was holding. Arthritis and years of punishing work had taken a toll on his once-strong grip, but his heart would not allow his hand to slip as he steadied himself further.

The painstaking task of getting each person to higher and dryer ground was finally over and Valerie, Sabrina, Jeb, and Tim grabbed the line hoisting Maria, Zack, and Brea to safety. The three collapsed on the ground coughing and crying yet very much alive.

"We will get you to a medical facility" Tim reported.

"Gone" whispered Maria with her head in the mud. "Gone. They're gone."

"No Mama, Daddy wouldn't let that happen" assured Zack crying uncontrollably.

"Ma'am, who?" asked Valerie. "Who's gone?"

Maria couldn't answer. She began hyperventilating and screaming with her face pushing deeper into the mud.

"My Daddy and my little brother!" cried Zack.

"You mean there's still two more of your family out there?" Tim asked.

Maria finally gathered her wits enough to mutter, "They were c… carried d… downstream."

As Brock, Jag, and Skylar arrived together on the shore, the team all looked at each other. They had saved the lives of this woman and her two children. There was no way they could get downstream fast enough. The risk of losing any team members would weigh heavily on the decision. They had almost lost three in the rushing water moments before. Plus, the task of getting the mother and the two children all the way to safety would be a challenge. After all, the water was still rising, and as unpredictable as water can be, there might be no way out before it's too late.

"Cap, there's no way we should risk this," whispered Skylar to Brock. "Besides, they couldn't have survived that. They must have drowned by now. Not tryin' to sound off but if we go on risking the rest of this team to find them we'll…"

"Quit? That's what you're sayin'? You *are* a mess man!" yelled Jeb.

"Quitting on people is not an option!" interrupted Brock. "I have never left a victim behind just to protect my own hide."

"But, what about safety?" shouted Skylar. "Isn't that in the training manual as well?"

"Hey, what does it matter? It's all gonna' blow up in our face anyway!" defiantly interjected Sabrina.

"Listen chic cool it!" scolded Jeb. "You 'aint gonna' bring me down. That kinda' talk will wreck us *and* them."

"Hey, dude *you* cool it! You got your issues too Mr. Perfect!" she quickly reacted.

Brock knew it was time to take control. He had never had to deal with such attitudes before on a rescue operation. This was strange to him and he knew that it could easily pose danger for the team as well as the fact that they would be aborting the over-all mission. But how had they come to this? Was it Brock's failing leadership ability? Was it his fault? What would his record look like after this decision? What about that plaque at the end of his storied career? Would it go from bronze to tarnished brown?

First things first – get the woman and her two children hoisted out. They quickly radioed for the chopper to come and pick up the first three survivors of this epic flood. The chopper moved in slowly over the river basin, then dropped a line down three times hoisting the three out of danger and up to the safety of dry ground.

"Chopper One, reporting all accounted for and now moving out. Copy?" came the all-clear signal from the pilot.

"Copy-that. Over and out," Brock answered.

Now, he surveyed the situation that was staring him and Team Alpha directly in the face. What was next for them?

Brock knew that there remained only two options:

1) They could keep moving downstream with full pack and gear as they searched the embankments along the way to find Don and Ben. Though risky, it was quite possible that they could find a path out of the basin downstream that had not yet been impacted by the swollen river. They could campout near an inlet and wait it out.
2) They could try to get out of the basin, up the mountain at about a 45 degree ascent, saving the team but losing the mission. This seemed like the most self-preserving choice, but it would be ultra-risky trying to get up the mountain. Plus, they would have to let go of most, if not all, of their gear.

Either way, they had to act fast. The river basin was filling up fast, leaving them little or no options for continuing downstream.

Brock was caving in to all the negative pressure and was hoping no one would notice. He had always prided himself on "not letting anyone see him sweat." Brock felt as though, being so close to retirement, and, with such a sterling record intact, he could ill-afford a messy report from his team when he got back.

So, he made his decision.

"Alright, we'll take the Land Rover out of here. There's no way those two made it this long anyway," he boldly exclaimed.

"Still think anything we do is gonna' be suicidal. We'll have to get rid of all the equipment to make it up that ascent," added Skylar.

"Got any other ideas?" Brock quickly retorted.

"Well, how 'bout *me* stayin' alive?" Skylar yelled. "I did well flyin' solo and I didn't sign up for none of these out-of-whack heroics."

"What's with you man?" asked Jag.

"What's with you, Jag? I, for one, would like to make it back home, if that's ok with ya'll and the captain here," answered Skylar.

"That about sums up all you men – it's all about you!" interjected Valerie.

"Yeah, well I, for one, know that I could make it out!" boasted Jag. "And, hey, we could always just ride outta' here on your back there mister grumpy pants," he added glaring at Skylar.

"I could get up that mountain with these two feet myself!" bragged Jeb.

"You men, bragging all the time. One of these days, you'll get a cold splash of reality hitting you in the face!" Valerie scolded as she withdrew herself away and closer to Sabrina.

"All of you wouldn't know which end was up if it hit you in the face," scolded Tim brashly.

"Shut up all of you! Just shut up!" yelled Brock. "We gotta get the gear outta the Land Rover before it's too dark. All this bickerin is givin me a headache anyway."

The team set out to pulling very expensive and significant gear out of the vehicle. They all reasoned that to go light was the best option. There would be no way they would make it up the 45 degree ascent even partially loaded.

"In all my life, I ain't never had to get rid of equipment before," lamented Brock. "This isn't a good omen and it just plain-and-simple goes against my better judgment."

"You think we're makin' the right decision?" asked Jeb.

"I'd be a wicked sally before this would have happened on my watch. This makes no sense, and yet…"

"We didn't mean to…" interrupted Jag.

"Don't care what you meant, I care 'bout what you do!" Now, this whole thing is a mess and it's gonna' take a miracle to get all of us outta' here anyway!" barked Brock.

Miracle?

Stranger miracles would happen soon.

# Chapter Four
# THE MYSTERIOUS STRANGER

U p popped one tiny head out of the rushing water, then suddenly another much larger head. Little Ben raised his tiny head above the water level barely breathing and coughing. He had been tossed back and forth and up and down by the immense pressure of the flood, but, by some miracle, each time would be propelled upward to the surface to catch a much-needed breath. This tiny miracle was surviving and his father, Don, finally caught up to him.

"Oh my God, Ben you're alive!" Don screamed over the noise of the waters. "Daddy's coming! Hold on. Almost there!

Don swam like an Olympic gold-medalist toward his son, Ben, scooping him into his desperate arms. Now lay the daunting task of getting the child to safety with one arm paddling against the raging torrent of the unforgiving, unrelenting river. Brazenly and with every bit of strength he could muster, Don hoisted Ben into the air and swam with one arm.

"Oh God help me!" Help me! I can't do this! Help me please. Help us!"

Don was losing strength fighting against all odds. He began going down under the water more frequently than he stayed above it. He was losing the battle. He had come so far pitting his best human strength against nature's fury and now, it looked as if this miraculous moment was quickly heading into the wrong direction – downward. Don could feel the pull and went completely under the water with Ben. This was the end. All Don could think of was how close he had come; his life passing before his eyes in a flurry. What if he had taken his family to the beach instead? What if he had been a better father? What if… what if he had taken more time for Maria and the kids? Why did it have to end this way, with so much to live for?

Suddenly, a large and powerful hand reached into the middle of the river grabbing Don's shirt and pulling him and Ben with seemingly supernatural strength toward the shore! The hand pulled Don and Ben both up out of the water and up onto the only remaining dry spot on the shore. Dazed and in and out of consciousness, Don, looked over at Ben leaning on him on the shore. He felt Ben's breath against his ear reassuring him that, at least, Ben was alive. Looking into his eyes, he could see Ben's eyes were open and a smile on his face.

"Daddy, Daddy!" Those were the two greatest sounds Don had ever heard to this point in his life! Ben was alive and ok. Don was alive too. Or, was this all a dream? Then, he looked up to see what happened, or… rather… who happened? Who had pulled them out? Who had the strength?

With the sun beating down behind the silhouetted figure, Don could barely make out the stranger's face. He was standing over them with a commanding, yet non-threatening stance. His eyes seemed full of peace, gentleness, and kindness. Don could barely make out his frame. He seemed well-built, but not to the point that he could have hoisted two people out of the middle of a raging river so directly. The man didn't say a word, but simply pointed Don in the direction of what appeared to be a camp site with a fire already burning and the pleasant aroma of food cooking. There were even two plates readied with one full of food and another looking unmistakably like a child's portion.

"What?" Don thought. "Somebody pulls us to safety, and then this guy has a fire and meal started just for us? What sort of person is this? Was he just in the right place at the right time?"

Don strained against his exhaustion and the glare of the sunlight to gain a better look at his amiable and benevolent care-giver, and then, suddenly, the man was gone! As he slowly edged himself and Ben closer to the fire, he looked again for this man or his back-pack, but there was no sign of him anywhere near. Where had he gone? Had all of this been just a dream?

Dream or no dream – they were alive! And, for the time being, they were safe. Now, it was time to get the two of them to warm themselves against the fire, dry off a bit, count their miraculous blessing, and hopefully, get back to civilization and, most of all, their family.

Hope was stirred inside of Don as he began picking up his drenched back-pack that had weathered the torrent. However, he knew they were not completely out of the desperation yet. They still had so far to go and had no idea of where to start. And, what about a rescue?

Would anyone find them? Would anyone even be looking?

The rescue team Land Rover crept along the riverbank, now free of most of the rescue equipment, pushing through the thicket and dodging flooded pot-holes and ditches. Though the terrain was treacherous, the vehicle plodded along as dusk was approaching fast.

Team Alpha was driving up a path that made tracks straight upward but at a dangerous ascent even for a 4-wheel drive. Their collective talents and training were being forced to mesh with a seemingly impossible scenario. Yet, they had reached the point of no return. Turning back, though a tempting offer, had evaporated with the flood's destruction of the few remaining levies directly behind and now below the rescue team. If they were to try to go back now, they couldn't. The path was gone! Lying ahead of them was "do or die". They could only go forward.

Somehow, that would play into the scenario that would ultimately save their very lives.

"This jalopy's doin' all it can to make it through this mess," exclaimed Jag stating the obvious. "Come on 4 wheel drive – kick in! Hey, Cap, maybe we could let out a little weight on this thing by getting' rid of Skylar and Sabrina back there."

"Always a joke Jag? Well, I think, you're a joke!" yelled back Skylar.

"Only joke here's yer riggin' skills dude," snapped Jag.

"With jokers like him around Cap, I don't see how any of us are gonna' make it outta' here!" Skylar reported as he looked for Brock to settle the situation down.

"We're gonna make it guys, don't worry. We can't go back anyway, all roads are gone." Brock replied.

"Yeah, and we might all be gone soon as well." Sabrina answered pessimistically.

"We might if I don't get a chance to take over this rag-tag operation. I would never have tried this. We could have made a makeshift zip line and propelled ourselves right over the river – if, that is, I were in charge," Tim whispered angrily from the back of the vehicle.

"Yeah, bet you would have gotten us in a worse mess," muttered Skylar contemptuously.

"I coulda' carried all ya'll on my back!" bragged Jeb.

"Hey, I hear all the under-yer-breath-chatter back there wise guys." Brock bravely reported. "Sit tight, and you'll see that we all will get out of this alive with a juicy story to tell."

"Yeah, how do you know cap?" asked Valerie

"Cause I got reports to fill out!" Brock quipped.

"Oh, how I wish we had just reports to fill out right now, bet I could handle this thing better," Tim whispered again.

As if drowning out Tim's latest snide remarks…

Suddenly, the unthinkable happened. The Land Rover struck loose rock and began quickly plummeting downward toward the river. Brock pulled up on the emergency brake with all his strength but could not stop the vehicle.

"Stop this thing! Put on your brakes!" yelled Skylar.

"I am! I am!" Brock screamed back.

"Quick Cap, quick, we're gonna' crash into the river!" screamed Valerie.

"Do something now!" yelled Tim.

The Land Rover suddenly struck the rushing river with a violent crash catapulting everyone and everything to the back of the vehicle like a bullet out of a chamber.

With terrifying domination, as if lifted up by an invisible crane, the team's vehicle was picked up by a wall of rushing water. The flood had risen and was swallowing everything up in its path of massive destruction. Team Alpha was now a rescue team in great peril.

The vehicle was pulled with tremendous speed and ferocity down river, striking rocks, and finally brought completely underneath by the commanding undertow of the water.

Inside the vehicle was extreme anxiety. Each team member was being tossed around in the watery grave that was their escape vehicle mere seconds ago. All of the years Brock Dunbar had served stretching out his hand to rescue others… and now, he was in need of rescuing himself.

And no one could hear their frantic screams as they plunged deeper into desperation and death.

Team Alpha's decision to abandon the mission and head toward safety had back fired. Now, everything spelled disaster and most likely – the end.

Don held his son, Ben close to the warmth of his chest. Ben, slipping in and out of exhausted sleepiness needed his dad to hold him tightly for both warmth and comfort. The fire seemed to be dying out and darkness was setting in just as fast. Though they had been miraculously saved from the river, it seemed possible that Don and his son might face a slower, more desperate fight for survival – the nighttime elements.

Would they be found soon? Was it time to set off and try to get back to civilization somewhere?

The stark reality was greater than his strength and endurance, and Don was giving up. The fight was leaving him. Where could he muster up the courage to get them out of this and even get them home safely?

As the embers of the fire were nearly out, Don decided to get up and begin to walk. Staying there, near the continuously rising and very unpredictable river was certain suicide, while setting out on a search for a path toward safety, though very challenging, looked to be their only option.

They set out with Ben riding on top Don's over-fatigued shoulders.

"Hey little man, we're gonna' try to get home, ok," Don tried to reassure his small son.

"Ok, Daddy. When can I go to sleep? I'm so tired." Ben replied.

"Not' till Daddy reads you a bed time story my little man. And…" he said mustering every bit of courage for that moment. "You can bet we're gonna do that. Just hang in there a little longer."

With an exhausted whisper, Ben searched for comfort through one question: "Daddy, does God know we're out here?"

Don had no answer.

# Chapter Five

# LESSONS LEARNED FROM A STRANGER

Hopelessness was quickly giving into death as the Team Alpha vehicle was being tossed around like a paddle boat in a hurricane. The members of this once-decorated and distinguished rescue team were nearing their final seconds and there was no help in sight.

With each gasp for breath and desperate attempt to hold to anything inside the vehicle, so many thoughts of what could have been were flooding Brock's mind as fast as the water racing around him. This was not the way he had thought he might die. He had always hoped to go out in a blaze of glory while rescuing one last time. He had imagined this moment with much more fanfare, not losing his grip on breath and life itself with a makeshift team of misfits and malcontents. Brock Dunbar was, after all, one of the most decorated men in the history of Search and Rescue Operations and now, he was about to go out of this world in obscurity and possibly never found.

There would be no bust in his honor, no banquet of thanks for all his years of sacrifice and service. There would only be questions; questions about his leadership; questions about the fact that he had led his final team into a flooded zone and couldn't bring them out alive. Instead of honor there would be the scandal and headlines to which he had so deftly steered clear for so long.

It was all over now. One more breath. One more surge. The end was now in sight.

Then, came the miracle.

Suddenly, as if the team had stepped over into the life beyond, a dominatingly brilliant light penetrated and flooded the vehicle carrying them upward into a vortex of power that rivaled the fierce power of the raging river. The strong force suddenly snatched the Land Rover out of the deadly grip of the water like an invisible super-crane. The invisible force was pulling Team Alpha... wait... to shore? What? How could this be? Was there a huge crane lifting them toward safety? But, if so, how?

Each team member, gasping for breath, looked with as much surprise as with horror. Was it all over? Was this Heaven? What was happening? Each one thinking out loud - "Are you seeing this too?"

The Land Rover was brought to settle gently on the shore as if a mighty hand had plucked it from the raging river and put a padded landing gear down just before impact. Though the vehicle was totaled from being tossed around the water and hitting the rocks in the water at breakneck speed, each team member was alive and basically unhurt. Team Alpha was in the middle of a miracle that neither one of them could explain. They began stumbling out of the torn up vehicle.

"Everyone ok?" asked Brock as he bent down catching his breath.

"Cap, my arm hurts, but I... I'm ok," answered Skylar first.

"I think we're all fine, Cap, but, um, a little speechless right now," Valerie added.

"Yeah, what just ha... happened? We were in the river one second and the next... it's like we were sucked up outta the water and... well, I dare not imagine by what or how," mused Jeb.

"Dunno, but I 'aint gonna wish fer getting back in the drink," Brock answered.

Then, they spotted something on the shore.

It was a sight straight out of a magazine. Situated conveniently on what seemed to be the only dry ground on the shore, was a camp fire gently blazing against the backdrop of camping equipment, a backpack, and what appeared to be an arrangement of perfectly placed food. Coincidentally, the number of strategically placed plates of food matched the number of stranded rescue team members!

Before they could take it all in, they noticed a man sitting near the fire. He was leaning comfortably against his backpacking gear and sleeping bag and was drinking hot liquid from a tin cup. The man looked up at the team as if to invite them over to the fire and seemingly totally oblivious to their recent peril.

Surely this stranger had to have noticed what happened to their vehicle, and how it was that one second they were going under for the final time, and the next... well, the next, they were staring in unison at him. And "hey, how'd that man get there anyway?" There was no path in or out except straight *up* the mountain while the entire river basin was covered in water! This one area seemed to be the only area that was not covered by water. Oh, but what a quaint and surreal sight it was! And, though it seemed impossible, this was no dream, and this man had to have some answers.

"Hello, um sir... did you happen to see what just happened to us?" blurted Jag. "We just got our keesters snatched from the drink dude?"

"Yeah, surely you saw something," chimed in Sabrina.

Without answering, the man simply motioned over to the stones situated around the fire – and invited them to sit down. Wringing wet and yet thankful to be alive, each member of Team Alpha inched gradually over to the fire and cheerfully obliged the stranger's invitation.

"You from these parts sir?" asked Jeb.

No answer came, nothing but a warm, understanding smile.

"You… um… see anything happen just now?" quipped Valerie. "I don't know, say, an entire vehicle snatched from the jaws of a watery grave at the last second… or something like that."

Again, no answer came. The man continued to eat and dish up more food for the weary rescuers.

"Um, hey, look thanks for the food and the fire, but… um… well, where the heck are we?" asked Skylar.

"Better question is, *who* are you?" the stranger finally spoke up.

"Um, well, we're Team Alpha, Elite Search and Rescue Team brought in because of this darn flood. Only problem, I think we almost died just now." Jag added. "But, I gotta ask, did you see how the heck our jeep got out of the drink like it did mister?"

"Sometimes, we have to see further ahead than *where* we are to *who* we are supposed to be," the stranger said. "The path for our lives is not always one that is predictable. Neither is the outcome."

"Uh, yeah, that's pretty mellow man," Jeb blurted somewhat contentiously. "But what does all *that* have to do with all *this*?"

The man gave Jeb a gentle look of kindness and then softly answered, "You'll see that it has *everything* to do with *all* of you before it's all over."

Questions and answers would have to take a back seat. They were safe and there was warmth and food in front of them. So, the team wasted no further time as they huddled near the fire and took the stranger up on his congenial offer of much needed refreshment, rest, and refocus.

"Grub's great man. Thanks a heap!" Jag complimented the man sheepishly trying to get some direct dialogue from this silent but oh-so-philanthropic woodsman.

"Yes, thank you so much sir. We almost died in that river and now… well, we're here having a hot meal. Don't know how it all happened, but this meal and this fire are true life-savers." Valerie added.

"Life-*saver* is what you and your friends aspire to be. But, are you?" the stranger asked.

"Well, that's kinda what we do for a livin man!" Tim answered somewhat perturbed at the focus of the man's question.

"True, but is that what you were doing? Were you a team about your mission?" the man prodded.

"What? You have to know that we got caught up in the same flood everyone else did," said Skylar

"True. That is the problem," answered the stranger.

"What do you mean?" Tim quickly asked.

"You all were trained and sent out by your superiors to accomplish a job. Did you accomplish it?" he went on. "I know you meant well, but to this point, each of you has been a team unto yourselves. Your training and expertise has been to serve you and your interests. The team and… the people you came to rescue, nearly lost their lives because of it."

"What? How do you know us?" asked Brock with utter amazement.

"Brock Dunbar – right?" the Stranger asked.

"Kick me with my own boots! How the heck did you know my name?" asked Brock with even more amazement.

"I know that you want what you always had before," the man went on. "And I know that you know how to get that back again. But, You won't get it back, unless you first…" the stranger suddenly stopped.

"First what?" Brock quickly asked.

"First *give* it up," the man challenged. "You must all give it up. You cannot rescue while you are drowning yourselves."

"Hey, don't mean no disrespect man, but we aint gettin' it!" rudely exclaimed Jeb.

"You're right, you're not *getting* it," said the stranger. "Any true rescuer who sees the need willingly sacrifices danger in order to save the person. Your choice to abandon the mission cost you more than you could imagine, to nearly include your own lives."

Turning their full attention toward each other, one by one, the team began realizing how they had arrived at the point that neither one of them sincerely wanted. They had all wanted to make a difference by joining the team – but forgot that their lives were about the mission, not their individual strengths or accomplishments. In fact, those were the very things standing in their way from doing their duty and fulfilling the mission, and it, without a miracle, they would have all died because of it.

"You know Cap, we were wrong to push you into making that decision back there," lamented Valerie taking the lead spokesperson role for once. "And guys, I was really wrong to turn on you. I should have appreciated your great talents more. It almost cost all of us. Forgive me."

"No, Val, we were the ones in the wrong," challenged Jag. "In fact, I'm the jokin' idiot that can't seem to see the seriousness of things. I guess I'm always at my best when I'm loose, but I didn't stop to think others might not be. Can't say sorry enough, Val. So sorry team. I think I get it now."

"No, I'm most definitely the one who caused the problem!" blurted out Sabrina. "I brought the whole team into funksville with my stupid negativity. Captain, I was so wrong to keep throwing a wet blanket on every move you made. Team, please forgive me and give me one more chance."

Brock Dunbar just kept quiet, taking it all in, savoring the moment.

Jeb jumped in as well. "Guys, my bad too. You know this thing wasn't always about a competition and showing up and showing out, yet, in my craziness I put myself *up* and let you guys *down*. Please forgive me team. Forgive me Captain. I don't want to always try to show people up, but especially you. You really are the best, and I'm just a stinker!"

"Yeah captain, you really are, and I know that I hurt the team the worst. My incessant complaining and self-preserving attitude paralyzed the team. Guys, I don't deserve to be on this team, but I certainly do want to help get these people out alive and maybe help get all of us out as well. Can you give me one more chance?" Skylar appealed.

Then all eyes turned to Tim standing silent in front of the fire with his back turned to the team.

"Tim, anything you have to say?" the team asked in unison.

No answer came. A prolonged silence from Tim added to the awkwardness of the moment.

Brock spoke up. "Ya know, in all my years a' goin' and trainin' and all I've done, I have never witnessed such a turn around on dime as I have today. I guess our near miss tragedy did its job. So, I am proud of you guys, and I too want to get on with the mission and get home safely. We're gonna' have to lean on each other to make it through. We'll have to go the rest of the way on foot... but, we can get out if we stick together."

Turning back to the stranger, Brock stuck out his hand to thank him...

But, to everyone's amazement, the man was suddenly gone! Nothing remained but the fire that was going out.

# Chapter Six

# GETTING IT AND GETTING OUT

U p ahead a mere hundred yards or so appeared to be a long, dry path leading to an open field. This was Don's chance. He had trekked so long, for what seemed like days, through the thickness of the Pine Mountain river basin searching for any sign of a path out, and now, finally, perhaps…

"Yes, it is!" he yelled with what little energy he could muster. "Hey little man, looks like we might just get you that bed-time story yet, if I can just… if I can just make it up one more time."

Don's son was lunging back and forth on his neck asleep and fully oblivious to the searing pain that cascaded throughout Don's body. Don was suffering from the injury sustained in his shoulders and back from being pounded by the rocks in the river and pure exhaustion from having carried Ben on his shoulders straight up the mountain for nearly 2 miles. There wasn't much left, but at least it appeared they might be seeing the light of day.

Then, just up ahead a fork in the path appeared. Which one should he take? Both were heading up but if he went down the wrong path for a long time, and it turned out to lead back toward the river, it would be the end of him. Both paths started out similar and yet both seemed to disappear into a thicket of brush that offered only confusion.

Staring at a major decision again, Don was about to go to the path to the left, when a familiar voice called out to him.

"Tough call, huh?"

"Wha, huh?" Don muttered desperately. "Oh, hi, you look… um… familiar. Were you just down by the river earlier today?" he finished as he gently set Ben down on the ground laying him on his soft backpack.

"Yes, and now, looks like you might be nearing the end of your challenging journey," replied the man.

"Wish this whole nightmare was over, to be honest with you." Don said. "Hey, never got the chance to thank you today for helping me and my son. I don't know what you did, but I think you saved us."

"And now, you need saving again?" asked the man.

"Oh, I don't know. Either decision I make seems like it will be the wrong one. That's all I've done this whole vacation, and look what trouble it got us in now!" Don exclaimed feeling ashamed.

"But, you're still alive aren't you?" asked the man.

"Yeah… until I screw up and make the wrong choice and doom my son and I. What does it matter anyway? I think I've lost my whole family. They couldn't have survived that river back there." Don sadly resigned.

"Everyone makes wrong choices, and everyone is in need of rescuing. But, it's those that admit they need rescuing, that seem to find the right path to freedom," the man answered gently. "You made mistakes, true, but you seem ready to right those wrongs and find your way out."

"Heh, yeah, understatement. But, if I choose the wrong path, I think I won't have what it takes to make up for one more mistake. Know what I mean fella?"

"Yes, I do, and that's why I am here to let you know that you aren't alone in this decision," the man replied.

"Not alone? Whatcha mean?" asked Don attempting to make sense of this dialogue with a total stranger.

Well, I have already gone down the right path ahead of you, and I can tell you, that path will lead you back to the road and back to safety."

"What? Really? So, you have already scoped it out?" Don excitingly asked.

"Yes, it's completely safe, and I have already… as you say… scoped it out," the man answered.

"Wow, thank you sir, thank you. We will do that. Here let me get my son up and we'll get going. Maybe you could lead us," Don replied with renewed excitement and vigor.

Turning his attention back to little Ben who was sleeping on his backpack behind him, Don woke his son gently. "Wake up Ben, we're almost home. This nice man here…What? Where did he go?" Don couldn't believe it – the man was not there!

His possible guide now gone, all that was left now was the decision, and Don knew which path to take, the one to the right. Confidently, he hurled his son boisterously over his shoulder and onto his neck again, and started down the right path.

He knew in his gut that this time he wouldn't screw it up. The man who met him along the path had already given him the confidence needed, pointing the right way to freedom, and now, it was up to him to bring them back home.

Back home… now that had a nice ring to it.

Dreams are so often crushed by the cold slap of reality as it hits you in the face. Nevertheless, dreams are also accomplished when we crash through challenging points of despair. Brock Dunbar had been trained to reach those "challenged by despair" all his life, and now, at his crucial moment of challenging despair, hope would have to come, not from his own hand, or his own training, or even his own gut-instinct, but from somewhere or someone else. He needed to completely lean on his team. Although very humbling, the whole idea of learning to listen to and lean on "subordinates" seemed to be working in the opposite of what he would have imagined. It was beginning to look like this was the very piece of his life that was missing all these years.

Team Alpha, now moving toward higher ground on foot, moved along slowly, but confidently. The bickering had stopped, and, for the most part, they began to look like a fully-galvanized team. It was a pity that they had made the decision so late. The mission was nearly fully compromised, except for the lives of Maria, Zack, and Brea. And, though they had done a near perfect job of getting those three to safety, they sure hated to be the ones to give them the news that they had not fully-pursued the father and little Ben, leaving them to perish.

"So, Cap, what's gonna' happen to that family we were supposed to save?" timidly asked Jag. "I mean, it really stinks that we didn't get 'em you know," he further lamented.

"Yer right Jag. I'd be a wicked sally before I ever let someone go without giving 100%," Brock replied with passion and remorse.

"Well, Cap, why don't we?" asked Skyar suddenly but with stuttering hesitation.

"Why don't we what?" Brock answered.

"You know, you're right Cap, we should get them folks. I would kick myself all over this mountain if we found them dead when we coulda' gotten 'em out alive," Skylar replied with renewed boldness and confidence.

"Are you suggesting that we go back?" Valerie asked almost hoping that the very thought of it would be quickly dismissed.

"Well, we're a real team now and I know we've been trained to do this. So we don't have any equipment. That's not the end of the world! Heck, Tim here can still rig up a rescue pulley from a branch off a tree just like old-school McGyver," replied Skylar trying to ease Tim back into the flow of social acceptance and propriety.

"Yeah, and Jeb could shimmy down a mountain like a greased flag pole," Sabrina bragged.

"And heck, Sabrina was smart enough to grab the one first-aid kit that didn't spill out of the vehicle when we went belly-up in the river back there," bragged Jag.

"Team?" interrupted Brock. "You wanna' do this do ya'?"

"Cap, we're in!" they all chimed in, all that is except for Tim.

"Tim, you in bro?" asked Jag slapping him robustly on the back.

"Get your hand off me slime-ball!" yelled Tim. "No, I'm not in. I was never in with you guys. You guys are nothin' but a bunch of goofballs to me!" he yelled storming off and away down another path and out of their sight.

"Hate to see him go," lamented Jag with a rare somber tone.

"What no jokes this time Jag?" Valerie asked.

"No Val, I really think we need him, and I think he needs us. Besides, you see where all my joking got us," replied Jag shocking most of the team with his sudden seriousness.

"You've changed bro," remarked Jeb.

"I think we've all changed," Valerie answered with an inviting tone rare to her as well.

"Well, guess that's what's been wrong all along with our team and why we haven't done what was needed," Sabrina answered. "When I came to this team I should have left my opinion and my way of thinking out of things. But, this whole near-death-suddenly-alive experience has opened my eyes, and I, for one want to be a rescue team that gets it right and on time."

"Well said," Jeb chimed in. "We are a team and we need each other, and we need Tim. Let us resume this Search and Rescue Ops by first getting back our guy Tim!"

"All right, let's go after him and then rendezvous at this point in exactly one hour," ordered Brock with renewed leadership confidence and vigor.

The team set out in pairs after Tim who hadn't gone far. They began yelling out for him as they went along. No answer came. For nearly an hour they searched down one rocky path after the other.

Suddenly, Valerie and Jag stopped as they heard a very faint moaning sound coming from the thicket behind them. The faint sound almost resembled Tim's voice. As they drew closer the sound became louder and more pronounced. It was Tim! He had fallen into a huge hole dug out as a trap for an animal. The trap had very sharp and pointed wooden spears at the bottom and Tim lay at the bottom bleeding from his side and back.

"We're coming down to get you!" screamed Valerie. "Hold on!"

The two teamed up and readied themselves to form a make-shift rope with long reeds from in the thicket. They had to work smart and very fast. Tim's groans were getting weaker and it was very apparent that he was cut bad and losing blood fast.

They also knew their need for the rest of the team so they called out for help as loud as they could as they went to work making the rope.

Brock and Sabrina arrived first to help – Sabrina brandishing her first-aid kit. The four of them worked feverishly to put the rope together. As they did, Skylar and Jeb showed up and began to work hard alongside their teammates. The team quickly and deftly lowered Jeb down into the hole.

Jeb dodged the pointed spears with amazing skill. His athletic prowess coming in handy, Jeb knew he had one shot to get to Tim without getting stuck himself.

"Hey man, we're here. Hold on bro. We're not gonna' let you go man," encouraged Jeb as he grabbed Tim and hoisted him over his shoulder carefully to keep himself from getting gutted by the jagged poles himself or further injuring Tim. He motioned up for the others to pull up and the two began their ascent up and out of the hole. With keen precision, Team Alpha rescued one of their own.

They laid Tim on the ground as soon as they got him up but time was running out. He was bleeding profusely out of his side and was barely conscious. He had lost much blood and the team was losing him.

"Come on Tim, you gotta' make it!" cried Sabrina as she and others placed what they could over the deep cut on his side. "We just can't let him die out here guys!"

They applied as much pressure as possible but still blood was pouring out beyond their abilities to stop it. Tim was fading fast.

Was this it for him? Why did he have to wander off? Why couldn't they get through to him? What would happen now?

"You guys need a hand?" asked a familiar and welcomed voice.

It was the stranger back at the fire camp! He had been helping them along the way. But, how did he get to them? And, why did he seem to keep popping up when they needed him the most?

"Where did you come from man?" asked Brock. "You know, it's awful weird that you keep showin' up bro, but we sure do need a hand. Do you know how to stop bleeding and... um... well, anything else that might come in handy right about now?"

The stranger didn't answer but simply went over and kneeled beside Tim. He calmly placed his hand on Tim's side and suddenly the bleeding completely stopped! He went a step further and gently placed his hand on Tim's head and suddenly Tim began regaining consciousness.

Then… he stepped back and said, "Now, I guess you remember what rescuing is all about."

With their mouths dropped wide open with shock and amazement, the team turned their full attention to Tim.

"Tim, we're so sorry we let you go like that." Sabrina said as she hugged him.

"Yeah bro, we're not a team without you. You had us reeeeeallly scared there for a minute." Jag answered with his renewed energetic tone.

The team kept up the reassuring until Tim finally blurted out.

"Guys, I'm not sure what just happened – it all seemed crazy and scary at the same time, but I am so glad to be alive and… um back with you." Tim answered with thankfulness. "I owe you all an apology and especially you Brock."

"Aw was nuthin' Tim, just glad you're still with us," Brock answered with a sense of relief.

"No really Captain. You are the commander of this team, and I… well I… I have a real problem with leadership, not just you. I have burnt so many bridges just 'cause I got all twisted up about myself." Tim lamented. "I'm glad this team is still together, and I cannot thank you guys enough for saving my life. I owe you all big-time. Let me start by getting rid of my jerk attitude and start being a real team player."

"Now, that's something we all can agree on," remarked Sabrina. "Ah, it's good to be back!" She hugged Tim suddenly.

"Whoah, wait a minute there sister. I might be alive, thanks to ya'll, but my side is still a bit tender," Tim abruptly reminded her.

They all had to laugh at the irony and revel in the miracle.

Again, the team turned their attention toward the stranger and again he was nowhere to be found. This lone backpacking phenom had seemed to change everything about this team. It seemed too far-fetched to think that this one man might have been personally responsible for pulling them out of the raging river earlier, but it was no stretch to note that he had definitely changed them as a team. Team Alpha had almost lost everything and now they were alive and well and most certainly on track with the mission.

Ah, yes, the mission. Now, they had to get back on that mission and get home safely.

With the path lying straight ahead and nearly straight up, Team Alpha began moving slowly toward the top of the mountain, being extra careful not to slip on the loosened gravel as they moved up.

"Hey Cap, we gonna' try to find that guy and the little boy now?" asked Jeb.

"Well, that's what we kinda decided before we almost lost Tim for good. Guess we should keep to that directive – sure," he replied reservedly.

"But, how will we know where to even start looking captain?" Valerie wisely asked.

"Well, we'd almost have to just about head back down I reckon," Brock answered with obvious hesitation.

"Or" interjected Valerie, "We could get back up the mountain and get a helicopter dispatched to their exact coordinates where we remember them."

"If we can actually remember where it was," said Sabrina. "So much happened and our world got pretty rocked back there for awhile. But, if the team wants to go back down I'm in."

"No, I think Val's got the right idea. She's not just a pretty head," remarked Brock. "Let's take that plan of action. I'd be a wicked sally before we attempt to get back into that mess again. We'd actually be doing the two of them more harm than good."

"We're with you Cap," said Jeb excitedly. "It would shorten the whole thing if we could get back to the road above this mountain and were then able to radio for help."

Unanimously, the team conceded to the plan Valerie introduced and began their strident journey up the mountain by foot.

Within an hour they had made their complete ascent up the mountain and could see just beyond their point to the paved roads ahead. Alas, civilization! They had made it! They had survived an impossible ordeal and had all come out alive and… perhaps just as importantly - changed.

This team of expertly trained men and women had lost their mission directive and nearly their lives as well. Their obsession with self-gratification and self-preservation derailed the mission but not their reputation. They had a chance at rescue operation redemption and they were walking through that door now with flying colors.

They all agreed that they owed their lives and their legacy to one backpacker who saved them when the chips were down. Who was he? Where did he come from? Would they ever know?

A rescue helicopter landed in an open field near them. They quickly boarded the chopper.

Above the noise of the chopper blades, Skylar yelled to the pilot, "We gotta' get back to our original position down in the River basin. There's a man and a small boy still down there!"

"What sector were you in?" the pilot asked loudly.

"We started out in Sector 6 East of here and down nearly by the bank of the river," Brock answered.

"Sector 6, you said?" the pilot yelled back.

"Yeah, I… I think so. We kinda' got turned around a bit and lost all our equipment," Brock replied hanging his head as he entertained a snapshot of the team's previous nightmare.

"Well, I'll take you down, but we just picked up a man and his little son down near there about an hour ago," the pilot answered.

"Really? Wow, Cap, bet it's them!" Jeb excitedly added.

The pilot described Don and Ben to the greatest detail.

"Yep, that's them, I know it," Jag added.

The team decided to go with the pilot's report and each one breathed a final collective breath together signaling the last pen-stroke on an epic disaster-laden, yet life-changing journey. They all began to wonder, though, what might have been, what could have been, and what would be in their future.

For Brock Dunbar, his illustrious career as a Search and Rescue Operations Leader had come to a surreal ending. He had originally hoped he would go out with superior decoration and decorum, but he could now only look forward to exactly what that career meant in the overarching scheme of things. What indelible mark would be left by a life such as his? What might his future hold?

For now, though, he was just satisfied to get back to his truck, his dogs, and his own little chalet. It was high time to take a sip of hot apple cider on the porch, lean back in his chair, and go to sleep dreaming of his life's next big adventure. Yeah, that sounds just right.

# DISASTER WAITING II
## SO, WHAT DOES
## IT ALL MEAN?

The preceding story was, of course, a fictional story, yet very much a reality in theory for where the Church, at least in America, finds itself. We are standing at the precipice of a cataclysmic anomaly of global proportions that the entire Church must be motivated and mobilized to deal with. With that event coming, what then will the Greatest Force on Earth choose to do?

This storm that's coming will place the Church into sudden "rescue mode" and, just like the Team Alpha in the first part of this book, we, the Church, have been trained and deployed to engage the collateral damage caused by the tempest. But, will we?

If it isn't already obvious, Team Alpha represents many of the reasons why we are not, in fact, wholeheartedly and with reckless abandon engaging the mission of global search and rescue. Each character on Team Alpha is a mirror and microcosm of divisions splintering the Church and distracting it from its rescue mandate.

Notice, first, the character of Valerie – *obsessed with relationship issues.* Valerie focused more on how she *felt* and especially concerning spurned or broken relationships than the mission at hand. She was greatly distracted from the primary mission of searching and rescuing because she was allowing her *emotions* to play a higher priority than her *devotion.* Valerie is represented by a larger group of "relationship-absorbed" Christians who operate on feelings and gravitate toward sermons or special events that tout "how to fix your relationships". It is important to do our best to love everyone, especially those in the Body of Christ, but we get outside of the will and blessing of God when we focus on "fixing relationships" so much that we forget to obey God's will and pursue His cause. Besides, many relationships are nearly impossible to fix and the best remedy for many of those "relationship squabbles" is a good, old-fashioned invitation to come and get involved with Christ's wonderful Gospel Advancing Enterprise – aka Search and Rescue Mission.

Then, there's Skylar – *obsessed with self-preservation.* He represents many in the Church who are self-absorbed to the point of missing the mission of Christ and the needs of people all around them. They don't realize that "playing it safe" over "obeying the will of God" can be one of the most dangerous things anyone could do to themselves and those around them. You may know some people like Skylar from your church who seem to throw a bucket of water on anyone who displays the fire of daring for Christ. The believers who were a part of the new movement in the earliest days of Christendom seemed oblivious to this kind of self-preserving philosophy and were sure to exclude excerpts of it from their Christian mantra. Their lives were not their own and, therefore, bargaining away earthly living and comfort and convenience meant very little compared to eternity.

Thirdly, there's our cheeky hero, Jag – *obsessed with feeling good and being the life of the party.* Jag mirrors those in the Body of Christ whose delight and distraction are the same – fun at all cost. They would most likely choose fellowship dinners any day over evangelism and outreach. The truth is, many of these people are not truly happy, though they seem to be on the outside. These amusement junkies mean well, mind you, but they seem to live in unrealistic optimism that fails to identify with those whose problems and suffering need identification and sympathy, not another slap on the back or joke. Now, don't misunderstand me, I believe in being lighthearted and full of optimism as much as we can, but not at the expense of the rescue mission.

Next, we explore the mindset of Sabrina – *obsessed with anxiety and pessimism*. Sabrina offers us a glimpse into the constricted and handicapped world that so many in the Body of Christ find themselves today – the paralyzing world of fear. Sabrina models hopelessness and gloom. When pessimism penetrates the Church, people no longer press forward but carry instead an "oh what's the use anyway" mentality. Lost and hurting people might be rescued if only these Christians who suffer from the agony of anxiety would allow the Great Savior that rescued *them* to unlock their personal fears and rise up to jump into the river of rescue with both feet.

Next, we take a look at Jeb, who represents *those obsessed with personal accomplishment and competition*. It's strange, but many leaders in the Church today mask this characteristic by calling their motivation – *church growth*, when, in actuality, it might be nothing more than a competition to keep one-upping their Church constituents. I think I identify with this character a little too much. Earthly competition has robbed me of Heavenly significance at times, and, although I have repented and witnessed a huge change in my ambition, I still periodically deal with this. Competition can be good if what we are competing for is the rescue of those perishing without earthly gain. Now, that sounds great!

Tim represents those in the Body of Christ *obsessed with being smarter and more significant than others*. They are the ones who dwell, if only in their own minds, above others, constantly putting their teammates down and even going after leadership to undermine, undercut, and even bring down. They see constant wrong in others while never seeming to find it in themselves. This obviously takes them far off the rescuing path, because they cannot see others for the mirror stuck directly in their face. Each one of these Christian "Tims" probably excels in establishing the motto, "Let there be no personal ceilings in my life!" This sounds good but actually masks three main problems: 1) Overt pride, 2) Church-wide disunity, and

3) Dangerously limited levels of community. All of these characteristics make rescuing perishing people nearly impossible.

And finally, there's our great team leader Brock Dunbar. Brock seems to exhibit an *unhealthy obsession of the glory days of the past*. He has been in charge for so long, doing things a certain way for so long, and relying so heavily on accomplishments of yesteryear that he struggles with change and with those who are not on his level. Some in the Church seem to be stuck in those glory days as well, wishing things were as simple as they used to be, not hearing the cries of those around them because those cries cannot be played back on a tape that they either recognize or desire. The new opportunities to rescue and do so quickly are lost in black-out sessions reliving glory-filled pasts.

While these characters certainly do not represent every church nor the majority of believers, there are certainly enough of them to muddy the waters of opportunity for the others and, therefore, drastically hamper search and rescue operations. We don't need to get defensive nor point fingers, but simply admit where each of us may struggle and get over our offensive ways to build the strong networking bridges needed to be one miraculous team going after one miraculous rescue mission.

# Chapter One

# THE SQUEEZE

Recently, the Lord gave me insight to what would be on the horizon. Very soon the enemy of Christianity, Satan, will be temporarily uniting two main forces to squeeze out every influence of the Christian Evangelical Church in America:

1) Secular humanism
2) Islamic Fundamentalism

The Lord illustrated to me that it will be like squeezing something until it pops sending fragments all over the place (Acts 8). The Lord will allow this in order to get the Church to reciprocally advance if indeed by bending its will to match its fundamental design. The Church will be splattered and splintered beyond "normal and traditional" recognition. This will bring sudden persecution, but also sudden last day comprehensive and culturally transcendent spreading of the Gospel.

The secular humanist movement will do its dead level best to paint the Church into a corner of bias and bigotry (as it already has) and simultaneously Islam will begin to appeal to secular humanists to help rid the American society of Christians and Jews.

The Islamist will appeal to a broad audience who will seem absolutely duped and even doped by the sheer bizarre radical agenda of the Islamic movement. In other words, while the secular humanists are pouring out their vile and unfounded hatred toward Christians, they won't even see what hit them – before it's too late.

Islamic radicals will get louder, more threatening, and more defiant in public striking fear in people. The moderate Muslim population will give in to fear along with the rest of society just as the moderate Germans did in the 30's to the onset of the Nazis. No Muslim will stand against his "brother" radical, and therefore, jihad and Sharia law will take stronger root pushing out all other voices.

Then, the much stronger force, Islam, will turn its attention toward the secular humanistic movement and the "the line in the sand" will be drawn offering the Muslims carte blanche to slaughter millions at a time, and thus total domination. The goal of this "squeeze" will be to have no Christianity anywhere in the United States in less than 25 years. It will become a death sentence to be a Christian and the Church will get drug through the thick blood and mud of this world with fierceness and ferocity.

Gone will be the memory of all the amazing Christian "shows" that we call service as unto the Lord. Gone will be the many Christian palaces that have adorned the landscape for decades. They will all be replaced by ornate mosques and gaudy temples. Gone will be the Christian eloquence that enjoyed placid complacency for so long. Pious rhetoric will not survive.

# Chapter Two

# DIAGNOSING THE PROBLEM

Matthew 9:35-37

*"Jesus traveled through all the towns and villages of that area teaching in the synagogues and announcing the Good News about the Kingdom. And He healed every kind of disease and illness. When He saw the crowds He had compassion on them because they were confused and helpless like sheep without a shepherd. He said to His disciples, 'The Harvest is great, but the workers are few. So, pray to the Lord who is in charge of the Harvest and ask Him to send more workers into His fields.'"*

Quick test for you: What was your split-second reaction the last time you saw on the news a report of dozens of people dying in a terror strike in Baghdad? Or what about the senseless slaughter of Nigerian Christians at the hands of the Boko Haram? Though our responses vary, they may help demonstrate whether we are still tuned into a heart of compassion or if we have completely turned a deaf ear and heart toward the desperate needs of humanity. If we do react at all, it's usually one of pity followed by sympathetic rhetoric, "Oh, I wish I could do something about that!" or "I feel sorry for those people!" or "Why don't someone help them?"

The truth is that these horrific events, though a world away and certainly far from our daily concerns, can offer opportunities for us to recapture the original passion for reaching the world that embodied the New Testament Church. Often these events serve as gentle Heaven-sent nudges meant to awaken our attitude and aptitude toward the Great Commission. In other words, it's all a part of a Divine Test.

Our Great Heavenly Master is offering us a glimpse into His heart-breaking world. He sees the desperate needs of the fallen world, and, having done His part in rescuing this world through Jesus Christ, now awaits our responses to His snapshots of world-events, beckoning us to come away from the filth of self-centered living. The evening news then is much like a flare sent up to bring light to guide His church into action. He is speaking through the BBC News and World Report and CNN anchors saying to His lazy church – "Come quickly! Get out of your easy chairs! I need you! They need you! They cannot wait!"

The Middle East is in an uproar headed for an upheaval. Millions of people are hitting the streets ready to take on powerful dictators. Genuine human rights are violated with thousands of Christians enduring terrible persecutions. Islamic radicals are spewing out apocalyptic threats while recruiting disenfranchised millions and starting terror cells faster than Christians can plant churches. Families being split apart, entire villages and communities suffering complete obliteration, and governments dealing out harsh laws to control the voice of the Gospel are just the beginnings of "birth pangs" throughout the world.

And what are the churches in America doing about it? Are they galvanizing and concentrating their efforts for world harvest? Are they mobilizing an army of sold-out saints ready to bring in the Harvest before Islam snatches the opportunity away? Sad to say, as I have witnessed, the answer is – for the most part - no. So much is being done and so much money being spent to beautify the cosmetic appeal of our church-buildings and church services, while billions of people are waiting to be rescued from the unbelievable tyranny of Satan's grip. We are investing millions of dollars toward renovations while throwing mere thousands at efforts to reach the Harvest. When I see this I just simply cannot be quiet anymore! We place bold posters on the walls saying things like "Outside these doors is your mission field" yet the people aren't getting it because, as my favorite lyrical assassin, Lecrae, in his song, "Send Me, I'll Go" so aptly puts it – "the block aint changed!" I guess it means that if you at least put your missional message on a placard somewhere you can erase the real burden of having to actually get up and go.

But wait…

Will we get it before it's too late? Will we take our responsibility seriously? Will we get back to the imperative task of rescuing? I think there are many great men and women of God and whole churches that would agree with me when I say that we *can*, we *must*, and with God's divine help - we *will*.

But we must remind ourselves of some of the important principles that, if genuinely embraced, can help us turn the ship around quickly before it's too late for countless billions of people who are staring hopelessly at the disaster that looms ahead of them.

# Chapter 3

# WE MUST RECOGNIZE IN WHAT *SEASON* WE ARE

### Season one and Two

*Luke 12:54-56*

*Psalm 1:3 / Galatians 4:10 / I Thessalonians 5:1*

So, what do the clouds on the horizon look like to you? Do you smell the beginnings of a major storm or is calm weather on the way? What does the spiritual, economical, technological, and social climate of our world look like today? What are you seeing? Are you looking? Are you concerned? Are there any signs of the times that jump out to you and make you stand up and take notice?

I believe that we have put ourselves into a state of hibernation while the winds of a changing world howl around us. As I notice believers today, I often see radical seriousness about their favorite sports teams, hobbies, and family events. While all of these things are important and have their place, when you compare the amount of time, talent, and treasure that we devote to those pursuits while throwing an anemic bone at world harvest, it demonstrates a terrible lack of prioritizing and a desperate need to look again at the signs of the storm that is looming dark and ominous on the horizon.

Whether or not we ascribe to the position I am taking, I believe we will soon have to come to grips with it and begin to make drastic and sudden changes. I only hope that people quit dying until we get it. I cannot fathom the numbers of people who will end up in hell while we sort it all out under the guise and pretense of "God's timing" and our "Discipleship Training".

It's time as never before to understand what season we are in.

## Season One - It's not a season of church-growth but kingdom advancement.

Just like Team Alpha being made up of individuals each pining for their own agenda, thus is the state of the Church as it exists in its splintered condition.

I am convinced now as never before that the number one way to reach the entire world the quickest is for Christian churches to become *kingdom-advancement-minded* instead of *local church-minded*. A large proportion of the Body of Christ still struggles with the problems of selfishness and isolation. It's easy to see yet not so easy to discover how it happens. Whatever the reason, we certainly see the effects: so much division, so much competition, and so much time, talent, and treasure spent on temporary things that never impact communities or regions, and certainly not the desperate world. We see many churches spending 70% of their entire yearly budget on mortgage for their oversized buildings and grounds and building maintenance. That number is much higher for churches that call themselves "reaching their culture" by spending inestimable amounts to make their worship experiences more appealing.

Another 20% goes to personnel including, of course, an inflated salary for the lead pastor and anyone who fits in with him. Then, after insurances and other miscellaneous budget items, there might be 2%-3% left for reaching out to the community or world-missions. I call that – throwing Jesus a bone.

Comparatively, if you were to look at the schedules of pastors of churches, you might be shocked. Most of their time is spent in three areas: 1) studying for sermons, 2) counseling members, and 3) attending meetings on either church-government issues or church-growth issues. Only one of these is a biblically stable alibi for a pastor's time. According to Ephesians 4:11-12, most of a pastor's time should be spent in preaching the word and conducting training and equipping for believers to be sent out to a lost world.

It's a wonder that we are making any kind of impact at all.

Ministry staff members have to spend extra time promoting themselves and appeasing big-pockets to keep their congregants happy so they can keep their jobs. So much of what they speak about from sermons, therefore, never stirs the pot or gets people out of their comfort zones and into the danger zones of where the desperately lost are. Or, as one preacher put it, "If there were more honest preachers, there would be more dead preachers."

Just recently, after discussing this with Jesus, He spoke to me something I had never heard before. This was His statement to me:

"100% of the time any believer takes the Old Testament to teach doctrine that stands alone it is in error."

He was showing me one of the roots of the problem. So many leaders are trying to get things done in a manner that appeases the Old Covenant. From the Old Covenant these leaders position themselves as "the priests" that speak for God forgetting that Jesus fulfilled the old system and set a new system in place that gives "priesthood" now to each believer. Not negating the need for teachers at all, but that they understand their place, not as those who tell believers what God has said, but those who point believers to find out what God would say for themselves. It then becomes the job of those who disciple to point those whom they disciple toward learning and leaning less on the leader and his or her teaching and more and more on the Spirit's leading. Then, in the corporate church setting, it is all governed by leaders who help keep it under the Spirit's control. Wow, how wonderfully revolutionary! How counter-culture! How controversial! Yet, how needed!

The New Testament trumps all of the Old and has the final say. Therefore, if we live by the full-gospel we are less likely to dive off into old systems that hamper our effectiveness and our appeal.

Church leader if you want to truly "appeal" to people, before you even attend that next meeting with your staff on "how to refurbish and make your building more inviting and look more excellent" stop, drop to your knees, repent, and go into that meeting ready to wad up the blueprints and start a true revival with your staff. Then, get ready to radically love and pursue lost people. You'll then be supremely appealing. Oh, and then you won't waste the hundreds of thousands of dollars that Jesus had meant for reaching hurting people. Jesus is the One to whom we all must give account.

## *Season Two - It's a season to rescue quickly.*

Ok, you're chillin' out at a pool with some friends sippin' on a lemonade and enjoying some much-needed rays. Suddenly, a small child of one of your friends begins to slip into the deep end of the pool. What do you do? How fast do you respond? Do you wait to finish your lemonade? Do you wait until you are good and sunburned? I mean, after all, you were there to enjoy yourself, get a tan, and take it easy, not to be the first-responder to a crisis. Anyway, it's not even your child, so what's all the fuss?

Now, contemplate this - what would all of your friends think about you if you just sit there and do nothing? Would they be very proud of you? I have a feeling you might not be invited back to very many pool parties, at least from the family of the child that nearly drowned with you mere feet away.

The point is that there are at least 5 billion people alive today who are slipping off into the deep end toward eternal hell and God has called His Church to reach them before they drown in the Lake of Fire.

On that note, I must add that many of those who die - die way too easily. What I mean is that over 2 billion people die of very curable diseases or situations that could easily be averted. So many of those same people die of things like malaria, cholera, or hunger, and yet it takes such little effort from those that have so much to stamp out these issues. We can easily share our storehouses full of food with dying children in Africa. We can easily set aside a little pocket change each week to buy some malaria medicine or mosquito nets for some of the millions suffering and dying from malaria (the world's number one killer). What we spend on an X-Box 360 video game, for example, could ransom the life of a young pre-teen girl caught in the nightmarish world of sex-trafficking. I know, because each month, our family does it. We have committed to stop talking about rescuing people and start doing it. And, in some cases, we have witnessed that our help came at the last moment before disaster would strike a village full of children. We have seen God rescue over 3,500 children from child-sacrifice and young girls from being sent to their "big-boss man in China" the day before it would have been too late.

What if we had hesitated? What if we had been waiting to get a better system or strategy in place? I shudder to think of it.

Most of us have seen the stats that illustrate my point. But statistics don't change our hearts. We need a massive Holy Spirit overhaul likened to that of the early church.

Due to the outpouring of the Holy Spirit, the early church in the Book of Acts grasped their first-responder role very well and went after it with reckless abandon. Many of them gave up their liberty and even their lives for this. They understood what it meant to be rescued by the power of Christ and did not take it for granted nor treat it as an option to rescue others.

And what about Jesus? What was His contribution?

Jesus gave the greatest example in that He being one person, albeit being The One Person sent from above, suffered and died to bring life to billions. Then, He turned to His disciples and said, "Greater works shall you do, because I go to the Father." In other words, "Hey guys, I alone have brought eternal and abundant life to billions by giving up everything. Think of the impact you all will make if you do the same."

One life – billions transformed instantly and permanently. Those billions that have received such could easily reach the rest of the world, IF they will, and IF they will quickly.

We, the Church should embrace the fact that our season of great harvest is now. While we continue to say that we are waiting on God, He continues to say that He is waiting on us.

## *II Corinthians 6:1-2*

*"Working together with Him, then, we appeal to you, not to receive the grace of God in vain. For He says, 'In a favorable time I listened to you, and in a day of salvation I have helped you.' Behold, NOW is the favorable time, behold NOW is the day of salvation."*

I don't know if you are fully convinced of my point yet, but I pray that it motivates you to get alone with the Lord and ask Him what you can do to change and get on board. If you stop and listen and tune out the rhetoric that you have read from Christian self-help authors, you might hear a tone of passionate yearning in the heart of God for a quick action on your part. He might just stir you enough to trade in your loafers for a pair of running shoes as you "shod your feet with the preparation of the Gospel of Peace".

# Chapter Four

# SEASON THREE AND FOUR

*Season Three - It's not a season of higher learning but falling on our knees.*

I have been a believer for over 24 years now, and have thoroughly enjoyed my life as a Christian. I have to say that being a believer is that greatest life anyone could ever live. Moreover, I have fallen head over heels in love with Christ's Church. I simply love the Body of Christ. The Body of Christ is still the number one most inviting group in all of history. We have excelled in each century so far above any other group in humanitarian exploits and contributions to social justice and change. The Church has excelled, as well, in living above the norms of society to offer stability in the midst of instability, pus so much more. Considering all the good that the Church has done, I sincerely believe that it's easy to see more admirable qualities than not. However, as history demonstrates, the Church could easily have done a much better job on a much grander scale. We missed tons of opportunities even though we did many good things. History does not bode favorably for the Church in some instances when we have chosen to stay in castles with moats all around us. We settled in, at times, to marinate in a world of theology that was meant to get us out of the castle walls and into the grasslands full of peasants and paupers. We even fought over non-essentials of our faith, and consequently missed seeing the teeming masses of humanity slip under our feet while dancing around our camps of particular thought. We *divided* instead of *multiplied*. And, we did it all while gaining more and more head knowledge. We became scribes instead of sold-out warriors. We hastened to debates on Christian topics instead of toward those bound by darkness.

The only thing that we haven't learned from history though, is that we... um... haven't learned from history. We often let the big one slip away.

Consider the situation of just one country in 2011. When I first began writing this book the entire world was shocked at the devastation of the country of Japan from a massive 8.9 earthquake, and even more the devastating tsunami that followed. In the wake of all the tragic devastation two nuclear power plants were facing meltdown, adding to the intense fear and suffering of the people of Japan. As I have been praying for and lamenting the loss of life there, I remember hearing through American Family Radio, and Tony Perkins. Tony recounted what happened in Japan just after World War II. The story revolved around comments made by General Douglas Macarthur, the Commander of Allied Forces in the Pacific. General Macarthur wrote home to his constituents that the country of Japan, despite their suffering, was open then as never before to missionaries from America. He saw countless millions of Japanese humbled by WWII and the devastation their leaders had brought upon them (remember Emperor Hirohito). They wanted fresh change and especially the Gospel.

What did the Church in America do right after WWII? Without knowing each detail, it is historically supported that we DID NOT advance the Gospel into Japan when we had the chance. Today, Japan is less than 2% Christian. We absolutely let the big one slip away, and today, after the alarmingly tragic events of the disaster in Japan, it is highly likely that 90-95% of those that perished in the tsunami and earthquake slipped off into eternal hell.

I sure hope that we do get it! I pray that we follow Christ all the way and follow through on all that we promise Him when we are emotionally touched. Get up and get going with the Gospel. Let's never let opportunities slip away again.

*Season Four - It's not a season for entertainment but for signs and wonders with holiness.*

Just like Jag on the Team Alpha, so many of us struggle with a lack of seriousness and being distracted by the constant need for positive stimulation, aka, entertainment. We cannot seem to stay still and wait on God anymore. Oh, before I pick up any stones, I am the worst. I revel in being a part of "what's happenin". In fact, I wrote my character, Jag somewhat from my own personality. I hate to sit still. I hate boredom and yet struggle to see the seriousness of life sometimes.

Ok, so this is a real personal struggle for me and for many, yet when it becomes the identity of a church, it becomes that much more challenging to recover. You see, we seem to be drawn to the idea in our culture that people will come to our churches if we entertain them in some fashion. I am all for doing everything we can to identify with our culture in an attempt to reach them. But, the jury is out whether we are, in fact, reaching them. Are we getting the job done, or just drawing a huge crowd? It might make a little less difference if we weren't spending such large portions of time, talent, and treasure to make it happen. We program our services so much to grab the audience before they "tune us out" that the very One who is waiting to "reach" them, is programmed out. The Holy Spirit comes to radically change their hearts and build His own "atmosphere" that connects to lost people, and we push Him out. Is it arrogance? I don't know, maybe so, or maybe just a wrong perception of how God changes the spots on those lost leopards. He doesn't change them by our super-awesome atmosphere-building cool services, but His Spirit punching them right in the very center of their dark, lost, wicked hearts and convicting them to run to Him for His salvation.

He is trying to get to them and yet our "smoke-screens" are keeping them away. They cannot even take a stab at repentance and change. They have witnessed a super-cool show, but left unchanged, un-impacted, and still searching. It's usually then that the enemy comes in and snatches the Seed of the Gospel that we "worked in" to our "show" by having a super-cool preacher "relate" to them.

Jesus had rock-star fame but not because He did things to be cool, not that, I'm sure, He wasn't the coolest cat around. He drew untold numbers of people (they might all fit into one of our modern-day stadiums) by four ways: 1) amazing miracles, and 2) kingdom teaching, 3) incredible loving kindness, and 4) pure, sterling character and conduct.

Now, I ask you, is that how we are drawing incredible crowds today? Are we so amiable, so venerated as our Master was? Are we seeing miracles following us and our outreach efforts? Are we teaching true Kingdom of God stuff that draws those multitudes of spiritually starving people?

I would add a question to this whole issue: Are we living lives of worship that attract masses of people to our joy-filled services? Are we living as such sterling examples of true holiness that make people thirsty for change? Are our services full of Heaven-directed praise from lips of sold-out servants that attract outsiders like honey attracts bees?

We don't have to do so much and strive so much and spend so much on esthetics in order to reach people. We don't have to climb down the stairs of compromise in order to identify with the people. They don't want to be entertained, they want to be set free. The husband that yells at and abuses his beloved wife needs to be set free from anger, not entertained in the midst of it. The wayward teenager needs to be set free from rebellion and enjoy true freedom in Christ, not be entertained while rebelling. We don't need to sing and dance for her, we need to cut the chains of rebellion off and rescue her. She is crying out to be delivered. The angry husband is begging to be released from the chains that keep him in depression, loneliness, and self-destruction. Oh, my dear brothers and sisters we must awaken to rescue. We have partied long enough. Attempting to rid ourselves of the wickedness of legalism, we swung the pendulum the other way. We don't have to do that.

# Chapter Five

# SEASON FIVE AND SIX

*Season Five - It's a season to stand up to the bullies.*

How is it even remotely possible that a thriving fast-food restaurant could help to usher in nation-wide revival in one summer? How did Chic-Fil-A in 2012 get thrust upon the global scene like a rocket shooting to the moon? One reason – the CEO stood up to the bully of homosexual activism and ended with a bell-ringing victory.

Christians are to be humble and loving at all times sharing with a lost world the kindness that exemplifies their tender but super-atomic-Hero. However, they are not to just lie down and die just to appease a few. Jesus stood up for His cause for which He ultimately gave up His physical life – yet knowing He would rise again very soon after and that He would reign supreme forever. However, make no mistake about it at all – the people did not win over Him and kill Him – He gave up His life for a powerful purpose that He knew had to become the very change agent for the people He came to save.

In other words, He allowed a very temporary battle scar in order to completely dominate the war! Jesus, though scarred, is the Champion. He is the Divine Dominator who dictates through loving, yet firm kindness. He didn't come to *hopefully* save you – but *most definitely* save you and take all your sins away. He came to completely take over our lives to empower us to save others. Therefore, we should stand up whenever and wherever we can with His mantle of kind and humble, yet very persistent and passionate public resolve.

In the county that I live in just recently a school board caved in to a one-letter pressure tactic by the infamous group Freedom From Religion, a powerful atheistic group bound by one resolution – stamp out Christianity and all signs of it from the entire United States of America. They want crosses removed from military facilities, Christian prayer removed from schools, and anything else they can dream up as they go along. This group sends threatening letters all the time to school boards. As a result so many schools across our nation are forthrightly caving in without even checking on the laws of their state, city, or county and most definitely without checking the very clear language of our founding fathers as penned in our beloved U.S. Constitution.

We don't have to abrogate our position as believers. We don't have to sit back while the world takes over every facet of society as we idly and timidly toast our "in-church" accomplishments with the champagne of apathy, over-indulgence, and pitiful historic amnesia.

What do we ever think the Eastern Europeans from the 1960s, 70s, and 80s might say to us as they watch it all unfold? What might the Germans from the 1920s and 30s say to us as they watch all that we timidly allow? I believe they would be pulling out bull-horns and screaming – "Stop the madness! Stop before you become like us!"

Anyway, all that the bullies are threatening can best be summed up as a collective – "boo!" Christians are being told that they must relinquish their rights of praying to Jesus or they will be… um… well… sued! That's right – sued or fired or kicked out of parties or whatever. I realize that not all Christians that are threatened cave in so easily, it just seems to be a society-wide scourge. I say, tell them, "Go ahead, sue me or put me in jail. I will never stop praying or preaching the Gospel, or standing up for righteousness!"

Remember those "timid creatures" called *the early apostles*? Remember what Peter and John told the bullies on that day they were told to "stop preaching this Jesus!" They were beaten just before they were threatened, and still their humble, non-judging response was – "Whether it's right in the sight of God for us to listen to you rather than to God, you decide, for we are unable to stop speaking about what we have seen and heard." (Acts 4:19-20) May I paraphrase for a minute? Basically, they told them to stick it! But, they did it in the nicest, calmest, most non-combative manner. I know that we, who are filled with the same Spirit, having come to the same Savior that they did, can do as much. Even if we don't feel like it, we must make that stand and, with the constant help of the Holy Spirit, we can.

## *Season Six - It's not a season for safety but for living dangerously.*

Why has the air of adventure and pursuit of noble quests gone out of the Church? Young men go to years of Bible School to learn how to orate from the safety behind the pulpit. They are told to remain quiet and meek and never step out to the forest of great accomplishments because they might upset a few apple carts along the way and offend people.

Jesus was the most offensive man in history, seconded only by Paul and maybe an occasional Peter when he wasn't sitting in his house contemplating Jew/Gentile controversies. If you think I'm making this up, just read the New Testament. Jesus was always telling people around Him that there were many who hated Him and were even trying to kill Him. Heck, Paul had to be lowered in baskets outside city walls to escape for his life!

I remember the day well. Our family was enjoying a fun and refreshing time together at an outdoor Jewish Festival in Memphis, Tennessee. The place was packed and the festival stretched to at least two acres of land. So, a conservative estimate might put the crowd that day at or about 2,000 people.

We had been repelling from 20 foot rock walls, climbing in and out of fire trucks, eating Kosher snacks, and petting sheep for about 2 hours. Finally, the time had come to go home so I began rounding up all of my six children. I try to be a good father, intimately and intricately engaged in every aspect of my family. I enjoy my role of provider and protector of innocent young ones and a precious wife. So, this day was no different. I had my two oldest daughters in the small petting zone and turned around to get the boys to move toward a large oak tree where my wife was gathering our things together. I turned around a mere 10 seconds when I noticed that there was only one of my daughters now in the small petting area. Julia, my oldest daughter, was at the petting zoo cage but Victoria was nowhere to be found. "No problem" I thought. "I'm sure she's over on the other side of the petting zone a mere 15 feet away." I told Julia to go quickly join her Mama and rest of the family at the tree while I went to get Victoria. Julia and I searched the animal pens. We couldn't find her. I began expanding my search to the other arenas of the festival and yelled back at my wife that I was trying to find Victoria. The search was turning up empty and it had now been about 15 minutes. My searching grew more and more frantic as the crowd pressed in all around me. Many nightmarish thoughts began to creep into my head. I had to compose myself and get to her.

After another 10 agonizing minutes, I saw a lady walking my way from the other side of the festival holding the hand of a beautiful young girl that looked just like Victoria. It was her! She was safe and quickly pulled her hand away from the lady when she saw me and heard my voice. I hugged her so tightly that she let out a squeal and said, "Daddy, you're gonna squeeze the stuffins out of me!'

Nothing at that point mattered to me as much as seeing my little girl again. She was now safe with me and I was very thankful. My most noble quest was finding my lost child. I didn't send someone else to find her or wait until my wife approved. She, in fact, was yelling – "Go find her AC, no matter what!"

I didn't care about how I looked or if I was comfortable or even safe. I just wanted to see my girl again. I think that the Lord is trying to get us to look at ministry this way as well. He sees so many of us doing everything we can to carve out safe and peaceful lives. He understands our need for comfort and safety, but He wants us to come to Him for those things and to live under His supreme rule. If we trust Him, we don't have to worry whether we will be safe or not. In fact, the safest place on earth will always be directly in the center of His will. We can be in the middle of danger, yet are safer than if we were in the protective bubble of our own invention.

# Epilogue - All is Not Lost

If, after reading all of this, you are experiencing conviction - good. Don't let go of that conviction and yet don't wallow in self-guilt either. We have a wonderful Director of Operations on the job and He is ready right now to take you by the hand and lead you to the next level of abundant living He intended for you. He is that "mysterious stranger" in the first part of the book, and He is ready to do miracles in you and through you.

Though disaster might be right around the corner, just like finding my daughter that day, there is distinct good news – we will find and save many. But, here's the caveat - we must choose to get rolling now.

Jesus is, after all, the Lord of His Church, and He will get her facing in the right direction. Through faithful and obedient servants of God, Jesus can and will launch His mighty counteroffensive against the enemy. Praise God!

We are sitting in a great place to turn it all around. We are standing at an open door that needs only a nudge from a strong shoulder of concerted, unified effort. Here we are. Here we stand. Ready, set, go. Let's launch and not look back. How about it? Disaster might be looming but so is the Church and Its quick response. You are part of that great response.